A Giant First-Start Reader

This easy reader contains only 49 different words, repeated often to help the young reader develop word recognition and interest in reading.

Basic word list for

Thump! Bump! Tiny the Dancing Hippo

a	I	says
all	is	sheet
and	it	sound
around	like	special
at	likes	stage
bump	look	that
but	loud	there
can	Mama	thump
cannot	me	Tiny
dance	my	to
dances	not	up
do	or	yes
down	Papa	you
gets	place	your
good	Sally	what
hammer	say	wood
hooray		

Thump, Bump
Tiny the Dancing Hippo

Written by Janet Craig

Illustrated by Diane Paterson

Troll Associates

Library of Congress Cataloging in Publication Data

———

Thump, bump.

Summary: A young hippopotamus drives his family crazy
dancing all over the house until they make a special
place just for him.
 [1. Dancing—Fiction.   2. Hippopotamus—Fiction]
I. Paterson, Diane, 1946-   ill.   II. Title.
III. Title: Tiny, the dancing hippo.
PZ7.P1762Th 1988   [E]   87-10933
ISBN 0-8167-1077-5 (lib. bdg.)
ISBN 0-8167-1078-3 (pbk.)

10   9   8   7   6   5   4   3   2   1

THUMP! BUMP!
What is that?

What is that sound?
It is Tiny.
And Tiny likes to dance.

Tiny dances up. THUMP!

Tiny dances down. BUMP!

Tiny dances all around.
What a good dance, Tiny!

It is good . . . and loud!

THUMP! BUMP!
"What is that?" says Mama.
"What is that sound?"

"Look at me," says Tiny.
"Do you like my dance?"
"Yes," says Mama. "But do not
dance up there."

BUMP! THUMP!
"What is that?" says Papa.
"What is that sound?"

"Look at me," says Tiny.
"What a good dance," says Papa.
"But do not dance down there."

"Do you like my dance?" says Tiny.
"Yes," says Sally. "But do not
dance all around."

"I like to dance," says Tiny.

"But I cannot dance up, down, or all around."

Sally gets a hammer.

Papa gets wood.

Mama gets a sheet.

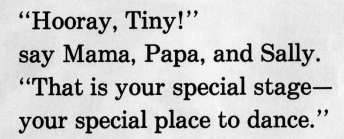

"Hooray, Tiny!"
say Mama, Papa, and Sally.
"That is your special stage—
your special place to dance."